Text copyright © 2021 by Karen Jameson.
Illustrations copyright © 2021 by Wednesday Kirwan.

Library of Congress Cataloging-in-Publication Data available.

ISBN 978-1-4521-8103-5

Manufactured in China.

Design by Amelia Mack.
Typeset in Losta Masta.

10 9 8 7 6 5 4 3 2 1

Chronicle Books LLC
680 Second Street
San Francisco, California 94107
www.chroniclekids.com

To Henry and Violet—with a hug-a-bye and a kiss-a-bye. —K. J.

To Matthew, my best friend and the love of my life. —W. K.

Farm Lullaby

By Karen Jameson

Illustrated by Wednesday Kirwan

chronicle books · san francisco

Neigh-a-bye lullaby
Slowly swaying rock-a-bye

Nuzzle nose, breathing deep
Plodding, nodding off to sleep

Moo-a-bye lullaby
Droopy eyelids flutter—sigh

Settling in, hoof to chin
Milky dreams come floating in

Baa-a-bye lullaby
Woolly lambs curl up close by

Fluffy, puffy, cloud-soft heads
Snuggling into straw-topped beds

Oink-a-bye lullaby
Drowsy, dappled piglets lie

Sinking in, mud to skin
Oozy, snoozy, drifting in

Quack-a-bye lullaby
Downy ducklings hush-a-bye

Resting, nesting, calm and still
Feathers cradle tucked-in bill

Peep-a-bye lullaby
Tiny fluff balls sleep-a-bye

Huddling, cuddling, dreamers cling
Pillowed under mama's wing

Squeak-a-bye lullaby
Blissful barn mice beddy-bye

Cozy, dozy, overlapping
Tranquil babies slumber, napping

Farm-a-bye lullaby
Field and barn melt into sky

Moonbeams shine on evening blush
Nighttime's blanket settles. Hush.